**CHECK FOR
AUDIO CD IN
BACK OF BOOK**

A PART OF

my quiet times
COLLECTION

www.myquiettimes.com

Please visit:
www.myquiettimes.com

A PART OF

my quiet times
COLLECTION

Title: The Tales of Wabby - The Present
Publisher: My Quiet Times, LLC.

ISBN 978-0-9793393-3-2
0-9793393-3-2

The Tales of Wabby
The Present

It was a beautiful day in Bunny Junction. The birds were singing, the flowers blooming. Everything seemed to be full of sunshine.

All except one little rabbit that is. Wabby was
sitting on the porch step with his teeth sunk in his
hands, just heaving a heavy sigh. He was doing
what we call some *stinkin' thinkin'*.

Now, *stinkin' thinkin'* is a way of thinking that is not very positive at all. It can sneak up on you when you're not looking, sometimes for no reason at all, and can make you feel, well, even sadder. Sort of like a big gray cloud that covers the sun for awhile, and all you feel is, well, stinky!

Now we all do some *stinkin' thinkin'* from time to time, but on this particular day, Wabby just couldn't seem to snap out of his blue mood.

So he decided to go for a long walk in the fresh air. Exercise always seemed to make Wabby feel a whole lot better.

On his walk, Wabby passed by Hobo Hound's house.

"What's the matter, Wabby? You're looking a little gloomy today," Hobo said, looking up from his yard work.

"I don't know," said Wabby. "I just feel a little sad. I want to play some games, but all my friends are busy. I wanted a piece of Grandma Bunny's carrot cake, but she hasn't made any for me for the longest time. Oh phooey-blooey!"

"Phooey-blooey is right!" Hobo smiled. "It sounds to me like you might need a special present to chase that *stinkin' thinkin'* away!"

Well, that's all Wabby needed to hear to make him feel a tad bit happier. Wabby loved presents!

"Is it a VERY special present?" he asked Hobo.

"Oh, yes, it's very special. It's one of kind, and there will never be another present like it in the whole wide world," Hobo said. Wabby was very curious to know all about his special present.

"Now, you wait right here, Wabby, while I go inside to get it for you. Now close your eyes and count to ten," Hobo said as he walked to his cabin.

Closing his eyes, Wabby counted carefully,
"One, two, three," all the way up to ten.

Then Wabby opened his eyes to find that Hobo had placed a beautiful blue book in his little paws. He couldn't wait to open the book up to see what was inside. When he did, boy, was he surprised!

"But there – there's nothing in this book, Hobo Hound! All of the pages are empty! No pictures, no words, nothing!" Wabby said sadly.

"Yup, and it's up to you to fill in the pages," said Hobo through his sly grin.

"Think about all the wonderful things that make you happy. You can put those in your book, one happy thought on each page. When you're finished, there will be a special present just waiting for you. Now, run along and get started," Hobo smiled.

Now, Wabby loved presents, but he wasn't quite sure about this particular present. He stared at Hobo for a moment and didn't say a word.

Then Hobo winked at him with a big funny
looking grin all over his face – almost like he was
up to some kind of trouble. That made Wabby
even more puzzled about Hobo's present.

All the way back to Grandma Bunny's house, Wabby thought about all the things that made him happy.

Now, I have to tell you, he started with a very short list.

Taking a bright orange crayon in one little paw, he wrote the word "carrots" at the top of the first page. He even drew a picture at the bottom.

On the second page, well, that's where it all came to a stop. Wabby looked at that blank piece of paper, but he couldn't think of another thing that made him happy.

Wabby was stumped.

Now, it would have been easy for Wabby to just quit, and go back to his *stinkin' thinkin'*. But instead, he did what he always does when he has a very big question that needs an answer.

Rubbing the little patch of white fur in the shape of a heart, right behind his ear, Wabby asked deep down inside himself:

"What makes me really, really happy?"

And with love and wisdom he heard:

It doesn't cost a thing to be happy.
A million carrots can't buy joy.
Its love, luck, and lollipops, and knowing what
you've truly got
That turns life into a marvelous toy.

Take time to smell the carrots.
Follow your heart and you will see.
When you believe your dreams are true
They'll be real for you.
And you will be as happy as can be.

Think about the things that make you happy.
Keep a happy list by your side.
Like riddles, jokes, and silly folks,
Bubble baths, and lots of laughs,

Funny faces, chicken races, Peek-a-boo

and smelly shoes.

Tickle tummy, chocolate yummies –
Yum, when they're fabulous bunnies!!

Suddenly, he had SO many happy thoughts that
Wabby couldn't write them down fast enough!
Before he knew it, every page of the book was full.
He couldn't wait to show Hobo Hound his pages
and pages of happy thoughts.

Wabby ran all the way back to Hobo Hound's as fast as he could to share all the happy thoughts he had written down.

"Well, hot-diggity-doggie! You filled up that entire book!" Hobo said.

"Yep!" said Wabby. "And you said that once I finished it, there would be a special present waiting for me!"

Hobo smiled his sly grin and sat Wabby down next to him.

"You see, Wabby, the book IS the present. Anytime you feel sad and get into a *stinkin' thinkin'* mood, just peek inside your book, and you'll see all the happy thoughts to turn your frown upside down.

Yes, sir, your present is right in your hands.

Be happy little bunny, and live in the present, and you'll always have magic right at your bunny toes!"

Later that evening, as Grandma Bunny tucked Wabby into bed, he told her all about his *stinkin' thinkin'* mood, and how Hobo Hound got him to put his happy thoughts down into a book.

"Yes, Wabby," Grandma Bunny said: "You're a very lucky rabbit." Then she kissed him gently on his furry little nose and whispered ever so softly, "Don't forget I love you," as Wabby fell happily asleep and she played him his favorite lullaby.

About the Author

Kevin Roth is an award -winning singer, songwriter, author, and performer. Known internationally as one of the world's most innovative dulcimer players and singers, his early recordings on Folkways Records are now part of The Smithsonian Folkways Collection. His voice has been heard around the world as the singer of the hit PBS children's television show, *Shining Time Station*, based on Thomas the Tank Engine.

In 2010, *The Tales of Wabby* was released as part of an original series of books and music featuring the original character, Wabby Wabbit. Wabby teaches children to make decisions about their lives by listening to their heart with love and wisdom.

His new line of books and music can be found as part of the *My Quiet Times* brand line.

About the Artist

Maggie Anthony was born and raised in Poland, where she worked as a film animator, background and sketch artist. Since she came to United States in 2002, she expanded her talents to include personal portraits, book illustration, and decorative painting. Maggie is part of the creative team for *The Tales of Wabby*, which she utterly enjoys.

The
End.